Feb. 08

I'm Going to Grandma's

Mary Ann Hoberman

Illustrated by

Tiphanie Beeke

Harcourt, Inc.

Orlando   Austin   New York   San Diego   Toronto   London

www.HarcourtBooks.com

Library of Congress Cataloging-in-Publication Data
Hoberman, Mary Ann.
I'm going to Grandma's/Mary Ann Hoberman; illustrated by Tiphanie Beeke.
p. cm.
Summary: A special quilt keeps a little girl from feeling
homesick when she sleeps over with her grandparents.
[1. Grandparents—Fiction. 2. Sleepovers—Fiction. 3. Homesickness—Fiction.
4. Quilts—Fiction. 5. Stories in rhyme.] I. Beeke, Tiphanie, ill. II. Title.
PZ8.3.H661mag 2007
[E]—dc22   2005005716
ISBN 978-0-15-216592-5

First edition
A C E G H F D B

Printed in Singapore

The illustrations in this book were done in
watercolor and acrylic on Arches watercolor paper.
The display and text type was set in Providence and Kidprint.
Color separations by Bright Arts Ltd., Hong Kong
Printed and bound by Tien Wah Press, Singapore
This book was printed on totally chlorine-free Stora Enso Matte paper.
Production supervision by Christine Witnik
Designed by April Ward

I'm going to Grandma and Grandpa's today!
I'm going to Grandma and Grandpa's to stay!

I'm not only going
to stay for the day,
I'm going to stay
for the night!

My mommy and daddy are taking me there.
I'm bringing my blanket. I'm bringing my bear.
I'm bringing pajamas and slippers to wear.
I'm going to sleep there
all night.

Mommy and Daddy both kiss me good-bye.
"Have fun!" Daddy tells me.
I promise I'll try.

"Just wait," Mommy says, with a wink of her eye.
"You'll hear something special tonight."

After they're gone,
we have cookies and tea,
Grandma's jam cookies.
She made them for me.
I have two cookies
and Grandpa has three
and I give their
new puppy a bite.

My grandpa's an artist. He helps me to draw.
He plays "Three Blind Mice" on his musical saw.

I'm teaching the puppy to give me her paw.
She's practically gotten it right.

My grandma likes dancing. She stands on her toes.
She's planted a garden where everything grows.

She has a whole closet of dressing-up clothes.
There's a bride one all lacy and white.

It's time to cook supper.
My grandma's a tease.
She says, "You don't really
want noodles and cheese."

I give her a hug and say,
"Please, Grandma, please!"
We both know she'll make it just right.

"It's bath time,"
says Grandma.
"It may be too hot."
I dip in my toe
and I say
that it's not.

But all of a sudden,
I miss home a lot
now that it's
almost the night.

I put on pajamas,
my most favorite pair,
but still I feel funny
and so does my bear.

Then Grandma sits down
in an old rocking chair
and says it will all
be all right.

"When I was real little,"
says Grandma, "like you,
one night I slept over
at MY grandma's, too.
I still can remember
as if it were new
the story she told me
that night.

"My grandma was YOUR
great-great-grandma, oh yes,
and when she was
just about your age, I guess,

HER grandmother made her
a beautiful dress, all flouncy
and fitting just right.

"Then when she'd outgrown it,
her grandmother said
they'd use it to start
a new quilt for her bed.

They cut it and sewed it with needle and thread
and each little piece was stitched tight."

"This quilt's Great-great-grandma's?
She made it?" I say.
"She did," Grandma says.
"And it's come all the way
from my mother to me
to your mom and today
to you."
And she turns out the light.

"Each patch has a story
of where it is from.
I don't know them all,
but I still recall some.
I'll tell you another
the next time you come."
Then she hugs me
and whispers,
"Sleep tight."

I dream of my clothes,
all the ones I've outgrown.
I dream they fly back from
wherever they've flown.

I dream I am making a quilt of my own
and my dreams keep me cozy all night.